Annie and Juneteenth

written by
Aletta Seales

Illustrated by
Artkina Celestin

Special thanks to all who provided feedback, support and encouragement.

Thanks to Dr. Sheila Bobo, Chairperson of ABENY, Inc. Education Committee, who served as an editor.

Thanks to my illustrator, Artkina Celestin, for her many hours of working with me to transform my words into visual art.

Annie and Juneteenth

ISBN 979-8-9863924-0-0

Book design by Artkina Celestin and formatted in Canva.
Text for this book is set in Art Nuvo Letterpress, Nickainley, Arimo, and League Spartan.
The illustrations for this book were digitally rendered in Procreate
using both Procreate and Retro MaxPack brushes.

This book is dedicated
to:

My daughter, Paulette Seales,
who sees possibilities.

My father Lloyd Whitmore
Goodwin, my first history
teacher.

"Mama, what's he saying?"

"Hush girl, I'm trying to listen and understand what that Union soldier is saying."

She responded, "Something about a decree from that President Abraham Lincoln."

"Mama, mama, who are all those men with him?"
"I'm scared mama. Master don't look happy."
He looks mad." "Hush and sit down on the grass."
"Don't even look up at master.
Keep your eyes down."

The Union army soldier, Gordon Granger, read:

There were about 2,000 Union troops, both Black and White, who arrived in Galveston, Texas on June 19, 1865. The army announced that the more than 250,000 enslaved Black people in the state of Texas were free by Executive Decree issued by President Abraham Lincoln.

The Union soldiers began posting
copies of the decree on trees
throughout the area.

Some of the Black soldiers who were former slaves that joined the Union army went into the crowd of Black formerly enslaved people and said. "So, you free to go."

"You don't have to work on the master's plantation anymore."

"You free to go."

"You free!"

Annie's mother looked at one of the Black soldiers and said, "Free to do what?" "Free to go where?"
"Am I free to send my Annie to school?" "Am I free to look for my other children that master sold away?"
"Am I free so that I do not have to work from sun up until sun down in the fields picking cotton then carrying it on top of my head to be weighed and then put through the cotton gin?"

"Free to do what?"

"Free to go where?"

Later that evening when the former enslaved people went back to their plantations and their places to rest, some of the plantation owners got together to discuss what they would do next. The plantation owners were nervous that without the slave labor they would not be able to profit from growing their crops of cotton and tobacco. Some agreed to offer the former slaves small parcels of land to tend if they would remain on the plantation and work in the fields. The former slaves would be paid for each bushel of cotton they picked and each bale of tobacco they delivered.

Annie's mother heard that there was going to be a meeting that night in the slave meeting quarters.

The women prepared food to eat. Annie was washed and her hair freshly wrapped.

When Annie and her mother arrived in the dark at the meeting place, they saw a big fire burning.

The smell of chickens roasting filled the air.

There were sweet potatoes roasting in the fire and white potatoes and corn. One Black man was playing his harmonica.

Some Black Union army soldiers were sitting on the ground smoking and laughing.

All Annie heard were the words,

"You're free."
"You're free."

"You've been liberated."

Annie's mother started placing her food on a blanket alongside of other food items.

The pastor appeared and prayed. He said, "Thank you Lord, we are finally free of the shackles that bound us. We are free to leave this place. Thank you Lord, for the food. And thank you, Lord, for the men who came here to tell us that we are emancipated." Everyone said, "Amen".

Then they began to eat. The food was delicious; the harmonica music was exciting. The children were dancing and jumping around.

One of the army soldiers took Annie's mother by the arm and lifted her up from the blanket and began dancing with her. Annie watched with a smile on her face and her hand over her mouth as her mother danced.

As time passed, many of the formerly enslaved people went west and traveled northwest to search for relatives that were either sold off, ran off or got their freedom to leave Galveston, Texas.
Annie's mother decided, along with many others, to remain on the plantation and work the land, accepting the offer of the former plantation master.

Some of the young men and boys decided to follow the soldiers out of town when they left. Those young men and boys wanted to become Union soldiers too.

Years later, that same army soldier who danced with Annie's mother on that first Juneteenth celebration came back and married Annie's mother.

Now, Annie has a little brother to carry to the special Juneteenth picnic celebration that the African Americans have each year.

At these celebrations, the grannies and grandpas,

aunties and uncles,

and mamas and papas tell stories of their experiences. This is their way of sharing the African American history and culture. The children still dance, jump up and down and run around.

And, oh, the food
is so good;
roasted chicken, a big pot of beans,
corn on the cob, okra and corn meal
and fresh berries.

Annie just smiles
as she looks into the brown face of her beautiful baby
brother born free on the land where her ancestors who
were slaves worked!

Glossary

Abraham Lincoln – 16th President of the United States from 1861 – April 1865 when he was assassinated. He led the nation through the American Civil War.

Cotton Gin – means "cotton engine". A machine invented in 1793 which quickly and easily separates cotton fibers from their seeds instead of it being separated by the hands of enslaved people.

Emancipated – Free from legal, social, or political restrictions, liberated.

Emancipation Proclamation – A proclamation made by President Abraham Lincoln in 1863 that all slaves under the Confederacy were from then on "forever free".

Executive Decree – An official order made by a leader or head of state such as the President.

Galveston, Texas – Galveston is an island city on the Gulf Coast of Texas.

Gordan Granger – He was a Union General during the American Civil War. On June 19, 1865, he informed the residents of Galveston, Texas of President Abraham Lincoln's Emancipation Proclamation.

Harmonica – A small musical wind instrument.

Juneteenth – A celebration on the 19th of June commemorating the emancipation of enslaved people in the United States beginning on1863. "Juneteenth, a blending of the words June and nineteenth, is an annual celebration on June 19th commemorating the end of slavery in the United States." (Lee & Low Publishers) Juneteenth is now a federal holiday.

Plantation – Large farm for the cultivation of cotton, tobacco, coffee, sugarcane, etc. using the labor of enslaved people, unpaid or low wage workers who live and work on the plantation.

Slave – A person who is the legal property of another person and is forced to work for and obey them.

Union Army – During the American Civil War, the Union Army (also called the United States Army) fought against the Confederate Army to preserve the Union.

Questions for Discussion

1. In the story Annie told her mother that she was scared. Why do you think Annie was afraid after looking at the master's face?

2. What was Union Army Soldier, Gordon Granger reading to the enslaved people and the townsfolk in Galveston, Texas? Why was he reading?

3. Annie's mother said, "Free to do what? Free to go where?" "Am I free to send my Annie to school?" Why is she asking these questions?

4. Where was the meeting held that Annie's mother attended at night? Who was at that meeting?

5. What foods were prepared for the Juneteenth celebration at the end of the story?

6. Who told stories at that Juneteenth celebration?

7. Why do you think Annie is smiling when she looks into the beautiful brown face of her baby brother?

8. How do Annie's actions make you feel?

About the Author

Aletta Seales is a retired New York City educator and administrator who went back to college after retirement to get her Masters in Library Science from Queens College the City University of New York. She worked in the Queens Public Library as an assistant to the children's librarian, coordinating and implementing projects for the after-school program. She volunteered at the Queens Public Library sharing her love of literature with children and adults. Ms. Seales is the secretary of the Friends of the Cambria Heights Library and advocates for libraries. During 2021 - 2022, she wrote a column, Friends Speaking, in the NYLA digital magazine. She is a member of NYLA/NYBLC, NYLA/FLS, BCALA, NAUW L.I. Branch and ABENY. Her philosophy is: "We are responsible for all children."

About the Illustrator

Artkina Celestin is an artist and self-taught illustrator who began her artistic journey at the age of three. She has worked as a freelance artist and illustrator for the past six years. She has illustrated a total of nine books for various self-published authors, as well as created a number of her own published journals/workbooks and coloring books. Artkina enjoys creating images that allows children of color (specifically African American children) to see themselves positively portrayed in books that tell their stories. In case you're wondering, her name really is Artkina! With a name like that, she was definitely meant to be an artist!

Bibliography

Barret, Anna Pearl, Juneteenth!:celebrating freedom in Texas, Auston, Tex: (Eakin Press. C 1999). Assessed June 2, 2021, Library of Congress. A biography of childhood and youth of the Barrett Family's social life and customs.

Branch, Murielle, Juneteenth:freedom day, New York: (Cobblehill/Dutton Books, 1998). Discusses the origin and present-day celebration of Juneteenth, a holiday marking the day Texan slaves realized they were free. Juvenile literature. Library of Congress. 394.263 Dewey number.

Gordon-Reed, Annette, On Juneteenth, (Liveright Publishing Corporation, 500 Fifth Avenue, NY 10110, 2021). www.norton&company.

"Juneteenth Celebration: A Local Legacy," Americanlibrary.gov/es/tx/es_tx_june_html.

Legislation S.4019-116 Congress (2019 – 2020) Bill designates June 19 as a legal public holiday.

Weatherford, Carole Boston, Juneteenth Jamboree, (Lee & Low Books, Inc., 95 Madison Avenue, NY 10016, 1995). Leeandlow.com.